FLy!

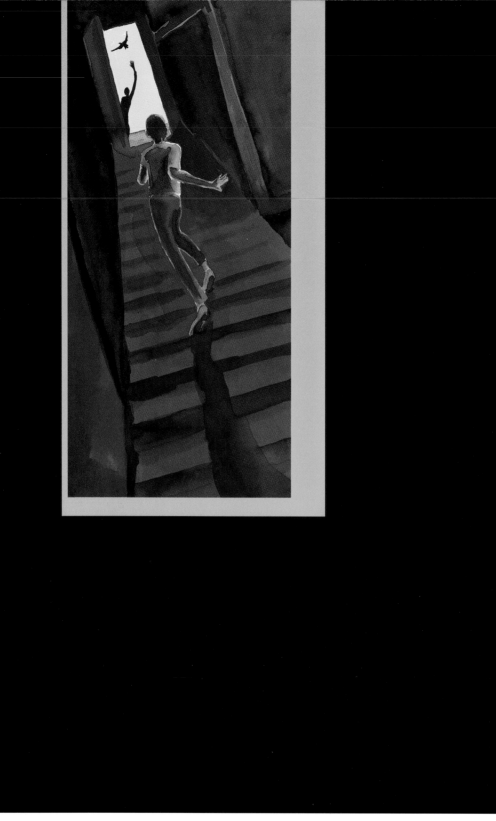

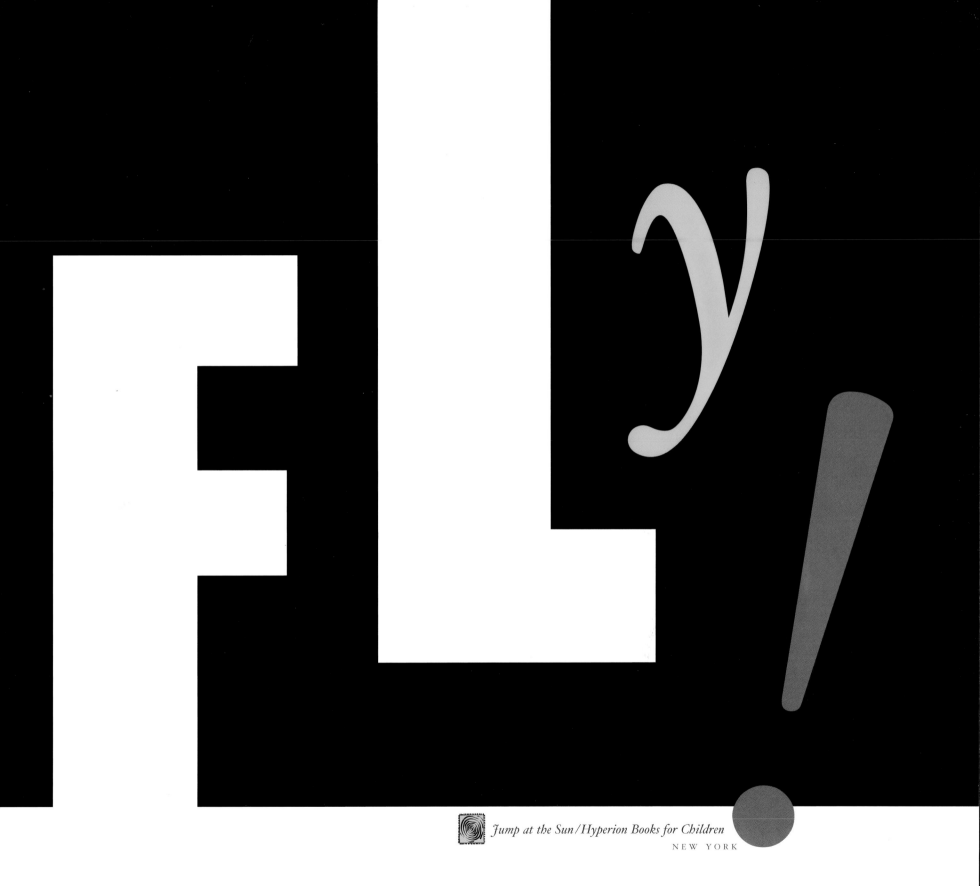

FLY!

Jump at the Sun / Hyperion Books for Children
NEW YORK

CHRISTOPHER MYERS

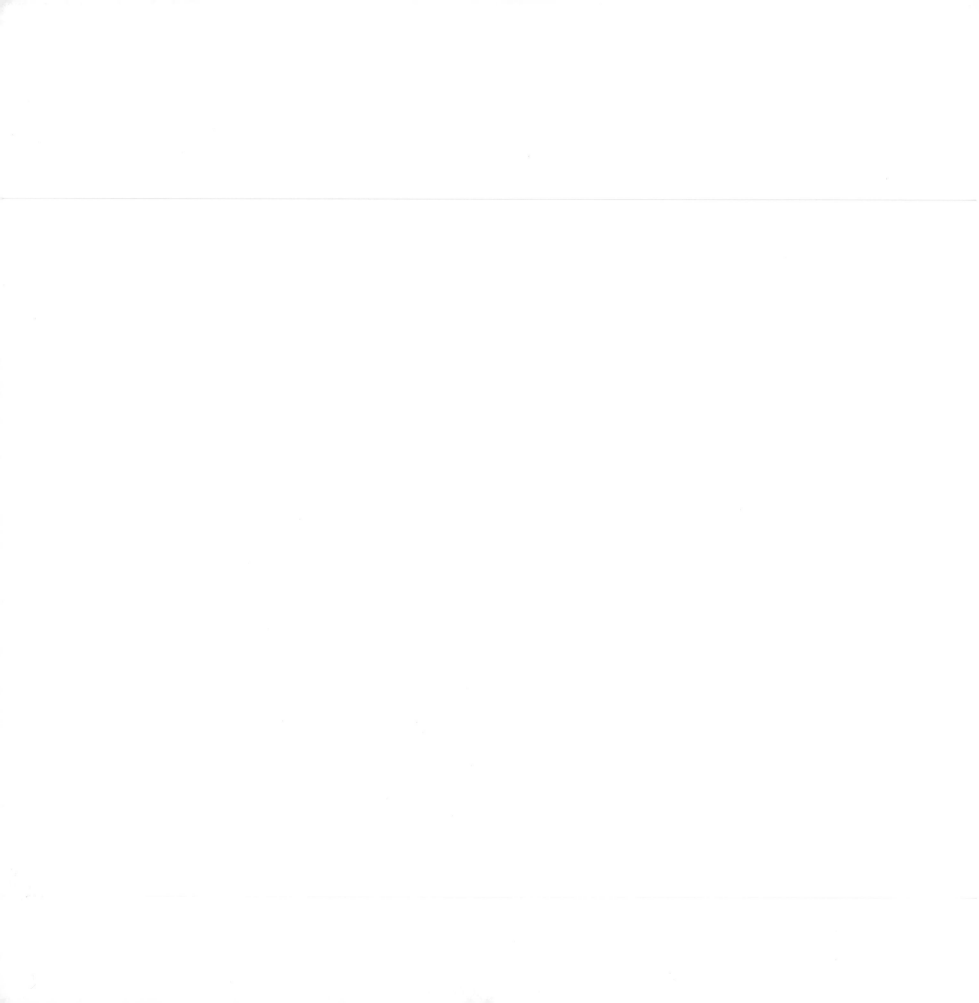

There are pigeons
on our building.

Every day they soar
from our roof to the
roof across the street

They are flying now,
a cloud between the
buildings, drawing circles
and patterns in the air.

A hundred black,
brown, and gray bodies
winging pictures in
the white city sky.

I wonder where
they come from,
a twisting river of birds
flying patterns
above my house.

M y window is high up,
almost near the roof,
just under the sky.
Standing at my window,
I can see everything.
I watch all the little people
in my neighborhood
running, shouting,
and playing games.

I wish I could go down there, but I am supposed to stay in our apartment, and not play in the street between cars.

Sometimes I talk
to the pigeons,
who fly near my roof.

"Hey, birds! Why you
flying like that—all crazy
bunched together—making
pigeon clouds?"

The birds never answer me.

But they spell letters and
numbers in their flight. The
bunch of them glides through
figure eights and zeros.

I write down what they spell.

8 0 S Q 6 9 C G

I don't know what it means,
but these are pretty much
the only letters and numbers
that they do.

So I holler out my window.

"What do you mean,
know-nothing birds?

8 0 S Q 6 9 C G!"

A voice like grits and gravy rains through the window and all over my case.

"Maybe you ain't supposed to know, because you too loud and too young, and you ain't listening."

I stick my face out the window. "Who's there?"

A man is hanging over the edge of the roof. He is wearing a white hat, brighter than the sky behind him, white as the mustache that smiles above his upper lip. His skin is dark brown, the color of church wood, and sharp at the edges.

His fingers are thin as sticks, and he is pointing one of them at me.

"Never mind who I am. Who are you?"

I stutter out, "My name is Jawanza."

"Well, Mr. Joe-wanza, you need not be yelling at my birds, because they are the onliest friends I got and they don't take kindly to no clean-headed, blabber-mouth boy hollering at them. Especially when they are flying under my melodious direction."

I guess I shouldn't be yelling at the pigeons. They just fly that way because that's what they do.

I look back at the man, who isn't there anymore. A silent line of birds stares at me from the space where he was.

One coos and turns his tail toward me.

I can't very well apologize to a pack of pigeons.

The man's voice still trips over the roof ledge.

"Can y'all believe
that Mr. Joe-wanza,
talking loud at you people
because you're flying?

What are y'all supposed
to be doing—swimming?
Playing basketball? Spades?
Child ain't got
no kind of sense."

He's one of those
neighborhood old guys who
says hi to my mom and me
every time we pass.

I creak up the stairs,
toward the door to the roof,
nervous as the light
that falls into the hallway
where the bulb has been
burned out for a month.

I can hear the warm
twittering of pigeons
in the sun.

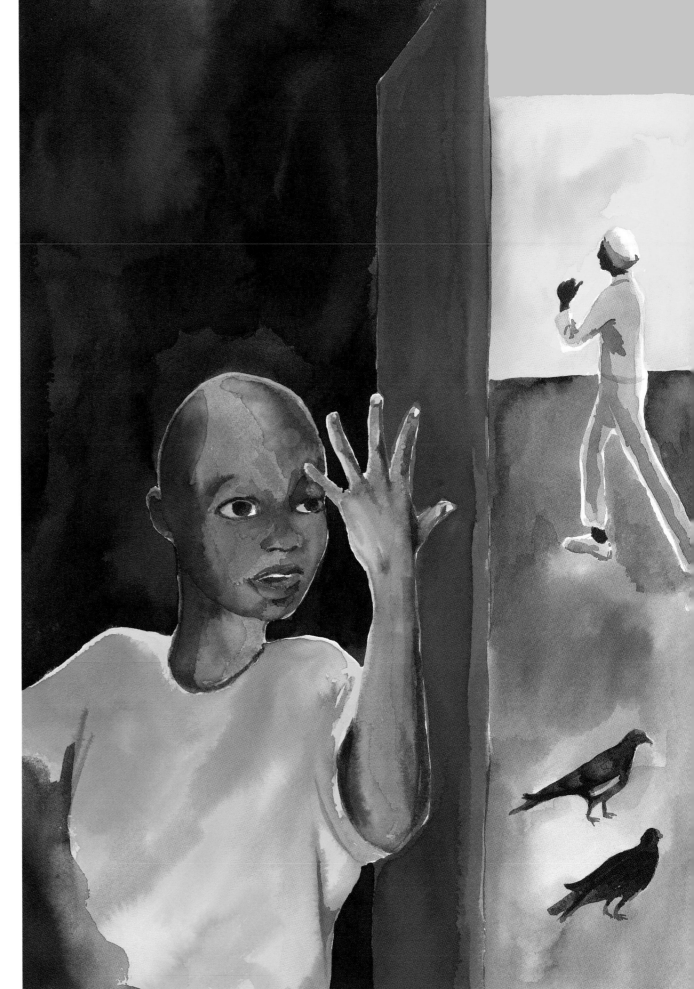

Behind the door there's the whole sky and a world of wings and beaks and the old man with stick fingers.

"Young blood, you come up here to bother the birds some more?'

He isn't looking at me as he spreads bread crumbs across the tar-covered roof.

"Why don't you go mess with your friends? These birds are my friends. Go play with your peanut-headed peoples outside."

I shrug my shoulders, and throw up my hands.

"But I don't have any friends, sir, peanut-headed or otherwise."

"Now that there is
a problem, Mr. Joe-wanza,
that's a big problem,
not that we can't fix it,
but that's no good.
I almost understand why
you're yelling at these birds.
You got nothing else to do.
I almost understand.
Almost . . ."

His eyes are smiling
at me as he lifts and cradles
a bird whose left wing
is hanging limp over his
thin brown hand.

"Is he hurt?" I ask.

"No, this is One-Wing
Jefferson, and he just
needs some rest.
Can you put him over
in that coop over there?
Take him gently."

The old man laughs
as he hands the bird to me.

He is chuckling and
telling One-Wing Jefferson
that he is going to be okay.
One-Wing curls into my hand,
easy as a feathered kitten.

I put the bird down
on the newspaper.
I think he's smiling at me,
a little beaky smile.

"Look, now you got two friends, boy, One-Wing Jefferson and Roderick Jackson Montgomery the Three, which is me."

He lifts another pigeon from the coop and holds the bird close to his stiff white jumpsuit.

"What kind of friend is a pigeon, though?" I ask him.

"Boy, if you don't listen, you won't learn nothing. God gave you two ears and only one mouth, because he wants you to listen more than you talk! A city bird is the bestest kind of friend to have. They don't tell your secrets. They give good advice. In general, they're good peoples."

I am still a little confused.

"But you can't talk to a bird,
and the bird can't talk to you."

"Boy, you need to
learn how to listen
with your mouth closed.
We don't need to flap
our lips to communicate.
Watch me!"

His head snaps back
and he spreads his legs.
He throws his hands out
to the end of his arms.
The sleeves of his white
jumpsuit cut across the sky.
The birds cloud into the air
around him and follow his
dance across the rooftop stage.

His fingers float
around his body.
His head swims in circles,
his hips jump, his wrists twist.
The pigeons are floating,
swimming, jumping,
and twisting with him.

Mr. Montgomery the Three
throws his wings open wide
as the city, wide as the sky.
He is flying, swooping,
soaring. He and the birds
are talking, communicating
in their own language.

My mouth hangs open
as he brings the pigeons
down from the air to their
tar-covered landing strip.

"Boy, close your mouth,"
he tells me.

I am filled with questions for Mr. Roderick Montgomery the Three, and some of them spill out.

"Mr. Three, how'd you learn to do that? Do pigeons ever tell you their secrets? Do they follow you all the time, or just when you are on the rooftop?"

He tells me that with time the questions will find answers. He says that he'll teach me the dancing bird language. Soon I can ask the pigeons for myself, with a shake of my head and tap of my foot.

I want to ask them so many questions, too.

Mr. Montgomery the Three puts his hand on my shoulder.

"Boy, before you can 'communicate' with these friends of mine, you got to meet them all. I know them, that's why they follow me. This here's Newk. That's Samo. Then there's Hip-Chops, One-Wing, and Fontaine. Know them all by name.

"Newk's got bebop in his blood. He be boppin' his head up and down when he walks."

A bird with a little tuft of feathers jutting from his head dips and struts in a circle, puffs out his chest, and whistles a twisty tune.

"Samo here is an artiste extraordinaire. Some people call what he does chicken scratch, but I see that it's art."

Samo, a wild, dark pigeon, flaps his way to the top of a wall covered in birdy feet marks.

"What does the fat one over there do?"

Roderick Jackson Montgomery the Three raises an eyebrow. "Be careful what you say to Fontaine, he's sensitive about his weight. He don't move too much, but he's got style, and that counts for something."

"Do you think I'll be able to fly with them tomorrow?" I ask.

"Nope. Probably not. But you can come up and I'll introduce you properly to some more of my friends," Mr. Montgomery the Three says.

"But I really want to dance with them soon."

"The problem with you now, Mr. Joe-wanza, is that you're too hurry-hurry to make the friends you're going to have. You got to take time with these new friends. But if you want to try with One-Wing Jefferson, y'all already friends."

I dance my right arm
in a circle. I swim my
head to the side.

One-Wing Jefferson
does the same.

Printed in Singapore
This book is set in Hoefler Text.
Designed by Polly Kanevsky
First Edition
10 9 8 7 6 5 4 3 2 1

Library of Congress Cataloging-in-Publication Data on file.

VISIT WWW.JUMPATTHESUN.COM